this
·little·orchard·
book belongs to

. . . .

. . . .

ORCHARD BOOKS
96 Leonard Street, London EC2A 4RH
Orchard Books Australia
14 Mars Road, Lane Cove, NSW 2066
1 86039 676 3 (hardback)
1 86039 811 1 (paperback)
First published in Great Britain in 1998
Copyright text and illustrations © Nicola Smee 1998
The right of Nicola Smee to be identified as the author and
illustrator of this work have been asserted by her in accordance
with the Copyright, Designs and Patents Act, 1988.
A CIP catalogue record for this book is available from the British Library.
Printed in Italy

Freddie goes to playgroup

Nicola Smee

• little • orchard •

It's our first morning
at Playgroup.
I'm excited, but Bear's
a bit scared.

Mum says she'll be back very soon.

She'll pick us up when she's done her shopping.

Let's play with the water first, Bear.

Now I'll paint a picture.
This is much too messy
for you, Bear!

This is fun!

At storytime, I'm so thirsty
I have three drinks!

Then we all rush around...

except Dotty, she's too tired.

When Mum comes to
pick us up, I tell her
we've been fine!